The Old Man of the Sea

W. W. Jacobs

Copyright © 2017 Okitoks Press

ISBN: 1979067082

ISBN-13: 978-1979067089

THE OLD MAN OF THE SEA

"What I want you to do," said Mr. George Wright, "is to be an
uncle to me"

"What I want you to do," said Mr. George Wright, as he
leaned towards the old sailor, "is to be an uncle to me."

"Aye, aye," said the mystified Mr. Kemp, pausing with a
mug of beer midway to his lips.

"A rich uncle," continued the young man, lowering his voice to prevent any keen ears in the next bar from acquiring useless knowledge. "An uncle from New Zealand, who is going to leave me all 'is money."

"Where's it coming from?" demanded Mr. Kemp, with a little excitement.

"It ain't coming," was the reply. "You've only got to say you've got it. Fact of the matter is, I've got my eye on a young lady; there's another chap after 'er too, and if she thought I'd got a rich uncle it might make all the difference. She knows I 'ad an uncle that went to New Zealand and was never heard of since. That's what made me think of it."

Mr. Kemp drank his beer in thoughtful silence. "How can I be a rich uncle without any brass?" he inquired at length.

"I should 'ave to lend you some—a little," said Mr. Wright.

The old man pondered. "I've had money lent me before," he said, candidly, "but I can't call to mind ever paying it back. I always meant to, but that's as far as it got."

"It don't matter," said the other. "It'll only be for a little while, and then you'll 'ave a letter calling you back to New Zealand. See? And you'll go back, promising to come home in a year's time, after you've wound up your business, and leave us all your money. See?"

Mr. Kemp scratched the back of his neck. "But she's sure to find it out in time," he objected.

"P'r'aps," said Mr. Wright. "And p'r'aps not. There'll be plenty of time for me to get married before she does, and you could write back and say you had got married yourself, or given your money to a hospital."

He ordered some more beer for Mr. Kemp, and in a low voice gave him as much of the family history as he considered necessary.

"I've only known you for about ten days," he concluded, "but I'd sooner trust you than people I've known for years."

"I took a fancy to you the moment I set eyes on you," rejoined Mr. Kemp. "You're the living image of a young fellow that lent me five pounds once, and was drowned afore my eyes the week after. He 'ad a bit of a squint, and I s'pose that's how he came to fall overboard."

He emptied his mug, and then, accompanied by Mr. Wright, fetched his sea- chest from the boarding-house where he was staying, and took it to the young man's lodgings. Fortunately for the latter's pocket the chest contained a good best suit and boots, and the only expenses incurred were for a large, soft felt hat and a gilded watch and chain. Dressed in his best, with a bulging pocket-book in his breast-pocket, he set out with Mr. Wright on the following evening to make his first call.

Mr. Wright, who was also in his best clothes, led the way to a small tobacconist's in a side street off the Mile End Road, and, raising his hat with some ceremony, shook hands with a good-looking young woman who stood behind the counter: Mr. Kemp, adopting an air of scornful dignity intended to indicate the possession of great wealth, waited.

"This is my uncle," said Mr. Wright, speaking rapidly, "from New Zealand, the one I spoke to you about. He turned up last night, and you might have knocked me down with a feather. The last person in the world I expected to see."

Mr. Kemp, in a good rolling voice, said, "Good evening, miss; I hope you are well," and, subsiding into a chair, asked for a cigar. His surprise when he found that the best cigar they stocked only cost sixpence almost assumed the dimensions of a grievance.

"It'll do to go on with," he said, smelling it suspiciously. "Have you got change for a fifty-pound note?"

"It'll do to go on with," he said

Miss Bradshaw, concealing her surprise by an effort, said that she would see, and was scanning the contents of a drawer, when Mr. Kemp in some haste discovered a few odd sovereigns in his waistcoat-pocket. Five minutes later he was sitting in the little room behind the shop, holding forth to an admiring audience.

"So far as I know," he said, in reply to a question of Mrs. Bradshaw's, "George is the only relation I've got. Him and me are quite alone, and I can tell you I was glad to find him."

Mrs. Bradshaw sighed. "It's a pity you are so far apart," she said.

"It's not for long," said Mr. Kemp. "I'm just going back for about a year to wind up things out there, and then I'm coming back to leave my old bones over here. George has very kindly offered to let me live with him."

"He won't suffer for it, I'll be bound," said Mrs. Bradshaw, archly.

"So far as money goes he won't," said the old man. "Not that that would make any difference to George."

"It would be the same to me if you hadn't got a farthing," said Mr. Wright, promptly.

Mr. Kemp, somewhat affected, shook hands with him, and leaning back in the most comfortable chair in the room, described his life and struggles in New Zealand. Hard work, teetotalism, and the simple life combined appeared to be responsible for a fortune which he affected to be too old to enjoy. Misunderstandings of a painful nature were avoided by a timely admission that under medical advice he was now taking a fair amount of stimulant.

"Mind," he said, as he walked home with the elated George, "it's your game, not mine, and it's sure to come a

7

bit expensive. I can't be a rich uncle without spending a bit. 'Ow much did you say you'd got in the bank?"

"'Ow much did you say you'd got in the bank?"

"We must be as careful as we can," said Mr. Wright, hastily. "One thing is they can't leave the shop to go out much. It's a very good little business, and it ought to be all right for me and Bella one of these days, eh?"

Mr. Kemp, prompted by a nudge in the ribs, assented. "It's wonderful how they took it all in about me," he said; "but I feel certain in my own mind that I ought to chuck some money about."

"Tell 'em of the money you have chucked about," said Mr. Wright. "It'll do just as well, and come a good deal cheaper. And you had better go round alone to-morrow evening. It'll look better. Just go in for another one of their sixpenny cigars."

Mr. Kemp obeyed, and the following evening, after sitting a little while chatting in the shop, was invited into the parlour, where, mindful of Mr. Wright's instructions, he held his listeners enthralled by tales of past expenditure. A tip of fifty pounds to his bedroom steward coming over was characterized by Mrs. Bradshaw as extravagant.

"Seems to be going all right," said Mr. Wright, as the old man made his report; "but be careful; don't go overdoing it."

Mr. Kemp nodded. "I can turn 'em round my little finger," he said. "You'll have Bella all to yourself to-morrow evening."

Mr. Wright flushed. "How did you manage that?" he inquired. "It's the first time she has ever been out with me alone."

"She ain't coming out," said Mr. Kemp. "She's going to stay at home and mind the shop; it's the mother what's coming out. Going to spend the evening with me!"

Mr. Wright frowned. "What did you do that for?" he demanded, hotly.

"I didn't do it," said Mr. Kemp, equably; "they done it. The old lady says that, just for once in her life, she wants to see how it feels to spend money like water."

"*Money like water!*" repeated the horrified Mr. Wright. "Money like— I'll 'money' her—I'll———"

"It don't matter to me," said Mr. Kemp. "I can have a headache or a chill, or something of that sort, if you like. I don't want to go. It's no pleasure to me."

"What will it cost?" demanded Mr. Wright, pacing up and down the room.

The rich uncle made a calculation. "She wants to go to a place called the Empire," he said, slowly, "and have something for supper, and there'd be cabs and things. I dessay it would cost a couple o' pounds, and it might be more. But I'd just as soon ave' a chill—just."

Mr. Wright groaned, and after talking of Mrs. Bradshaw as though she were already his mother-in-law, produced the money. His instructions as to economy lasted almost up to the moment when he stood with Bella outside the shop on the following evening and watched the couple go off.

"It's wonderful how well they get on together," said Bella, as they re-entered the shop and passed into the parlour. "I've never seen mother take to anybody so quick as she has to him."

"I hope you like him, too," said Mr. Wright.

"He's a dear," said Bella. "Fancy having all that money. I wonder what it feels like?"

"I suppose I shall know some day," said the young man, slowly; "but it won't be much good to me unless——"

"Unless?" said Bella, after a pause.

"Unless it gives me what I want," replied the other. "I'd sooner be a poor man and married to the girl I love, than a millionaire."

Miss Bradshaw stole an uneasy glance at his somewhat sallow features, and became thoughtful.

"It's no good having diamonds and motor-cars and that sort of thing unless you have somebody to share them with," pursued Mr. Wright.

Miss Bradshaw's eyes sparkled, and at that moment the shop-bell tinkled and a lively whistle sounded. She rose and went into the shop, and Mr. Wright settled back in his chair and scowled darkly as he saw the intruder.

"Good evening," said the latter. "I want a sixpenny smoke for twopence, please. How are we this evening? Sitting up and taking nourishment?"

Miss Bradshaw told him to behave himself.

"Always do," said the young man. "That's why I can never get anybody to play with. I had such an awful dream about you last night that I couldn't rest till I saw you. Awful it was."

"What was it?" inquired Miss Bradshaw.

"Dreamt you were married," said Mr. Hills, smiling at her.

Miss Bradshaw tossed her head. "Who to, pray?" she inquired.

"Me," said Mr. Hills, simply. "I woke up in a cold perspiration. Halloa! is that Georgie in there? How are you, George? Better?"

"I'm all right," said Mr. Wright, with dignity, as the other hooked the door open with his stick and nodded at him.

"Well, why don't you look it?" demanded the lively Mr. Hills. "Have you got your feet wet, or what?"

"Oh, be quiet," said Miss Bradshaw, smiling at him.

"Right-o," said Mr. Hills, dropping into a chair by the counter and caressing his moustache. "But you wouldn't speak to me like that if you knew what a terrible day I've had."

"What have you been doing?" asked the girl.

"Working," said the other, with a huge sigh. "Where's the millionaire? I came round on purpose to have a look at him."

"Him and mother have gone to the Empire?" said Miss Bradshaw.

Mr. Hills gave three long, penetrating whistles, and then, placing his cigar with great care on the counter, hid his face in a huge handkerchief. Miss Bradshaw, glanced from him to the frowning Mr. Wright, and then, entering the parlour, closed the door with a bang. Mr. Hills took the hint, and with a somewhat thoughtful grin departed.

He came in next evening for another cigar, and heard all that there was to hear about the Empire. Mrs. Bradshaw would have treated him but coldly, but the innocent Mr. Kemp, charmed by his manner, paid him great attention.

"He's just like what I was at his age," he said. "Lively."

"I'm not a patch on you," said Mr. Hills, edging his way by slow degrees into the parlour. "I don't take young ladies to the Empire. Were you telling me you came over here to get married, or did I dream it?"

"'Ark at him," said the blushing Mr. Kemp, as Mrs. Bradshaw shook her head at the offender and told him to behave himself.

14

"He's a man any woman might be happy with," said Mr. Hills. "He never knows how much there is in his trousers-pocket. Fancy sewing on buttons for a man like that. Gold-mining ain't in it."

Mrs. Bradshaw shook her head at him again, and Mr. Hills, after apologizing to her for revealing her innermost thoughts before the most guileless of men, began to question Mr. Kemp as to the prospects of a bright and energetic young man, with a distaste for work, in New Zealand. The audience listened with keen attention to the replies, the only disturbing factor being a cough of Mr. Wright's, which became more and more troublesome as the evening wore on. By the time uncle and nephew rose to depart the latter was so hoarse that he could scarcely speak.

"Why didn't you tell 'em you had got a letter calling you home, as I told you?" he vociferated, as soon as they were clear of the shop.

"I—I forgot it," said the old man.

"Forgot it!" repeated the incensed Mr. Wright.

"What did you think I was coughing like that for—fun?"

"I forgot it," said the old man, doggedly. "Besides, if you take my advice, you'd better let me stay a little longer to make sure of things."

Mr. Wright laughed disagreeably. "I dare say," he said; "but I am managing this affair, not you. Now, you go round to-morrow afternoon and tell them you're off. D'ye hear? D'ye think I'm made of money? And what do you mean by making such a fuss of that fool, Charlie Hills? You know he is after Bella."

He walked the rest of the way home in indignant silence, and, after giving minute instructions to Mr. Kemp next morning at breakfast, went off to work in a more cheerful frame of mind. Mr. Kemp was out when he returned, and after making his toilet he followed him to Mrs. Bradshaw's.

To his annoyance, he found Mr. Hills there again; and, moreover, it soon became clear to him that Mr. Kemp had said nothing about his approaching departure. Coughs and scowls passed unheeded, and at last in a hesitating voice, he broached the subject himself. There was a general chorus of lamentation.

"I hadn't got the heart to tell you," said Mr. Kemp. "I don't know when I've been so happy."

"But you haven't got to go back immediate," said Mrs. Bradshaw.

"To-morrow," said Mr. Wright, before the old man could reply. "Business."

"Must you go," said Mrs. Bradshaw.

Mr. Kemp smiled feebly. "I suppose I ought to," he replied, in a hesitating voice.

"Take my tip and give yourself a bit of a holiday before you go back," urged Mr. Hills.

"Just for a few days," pleaded Bella.

"To please us," said Mrs. Bradshaw. "Think 'ow George'll miss you."

"Lay hold of him and don't let him go," said Mr. Hills.

He took Mr. Kemp round the waist, and the laughing Bella and her mother each secured an arm. An appeal to Mr. Wright to secure his legs passed unheeded.

"We don't let you go till you promise," said Mrs. Bradshaw.

Mr. Kemp smiled and shook his head. "Promise?" said Bella.

"Well, well," said Mr. Kemp; "p'r'aps——"

"He must go back," shouted the alarmed Mr. Wright.

"Let him speak for himself," exclaimed Bella, indignantly.

"Just another week then," said Mr. Kemp. "It's no good having money if I can't please myself."

"A week!" shouted Mr. Wright, almost beside himself with rage and dismay. "A week! Another week! Why, you told me——"

"Oh, don't listen to him," said Mrs. Bradshaw. "Croaker! It's his own business, ain't it? And he knows best, don't he? What's it got to do with you?"

She patted Mr. Kemp's hand; Mr. Kemp patted back, and with his disengaged hand helped himself to a glass of beer—the fourth—and beamed in a friendly fashion upon the company.

"George!" he said, suddenly.

"Yes," said Mr. Wright, in a harsh voice.

"Did you think to bring my pocket-book along with you?"

"No," said Mr. Wright, sharply; "I didn't."

"Tt-tt," said the old man, with a gesture of annoyance. "Well, lend me a couple of pounds, then, or else run back and fetch my pocket-book," he added, with a sly grin.

Mr. Wright's face worked with impotent fury. "What— what—do you—want it for?" he gasped.

Mrs. Bradshaw's "Well! Well!" seemed to sum up the general feeling; Mr. Kemp, shaking his head, eyed him with gentle reproach.

"Me and Mrs. Bradshaw are going to gave another evening out," he said, quietly. "I've only got a few more days, and I must make hay while the sun shines."

To Mr. Wright the room seemed to revolve slowly on its axis, but, regaining his self-possession by a supreme effort, he took out his purse and produced the amount. Mrs. Bradshaw, after a few feminine protestations, went upstairs to put her bonnet on.

"And you can go and fetch a hansom-cab, George, while she's a-doing of it," said Mr. Kemp. "Pick out a good 'orse—spotted-grey, if you can."

Mr. Wright arose and, departing with a suddenness that was almost startling, exploded harmlessly in front of the barber's, next door but one. Then with lagging steps he went in search of the shabbiest cab and oldest horse he could find.

"Thankee, my boy," said Mr. Kemp, bluffly, as he helped Mrs. Bradshaw in and stood with his foot on the step. "By the way, you had better go back and lock my pocket-book up. I left it on the washstand, and there's best part of a thousand pounds in it. You can take fifty for yourself to buy smokes with."

There was a murmur of admiration, and Mr. Wright, with a frantic attempt to keep up appearances, tried to thank him, but in vain. Long after the cab had rolled away he stood on the pavement trying to think out a position which was rapidly becoming unendurable. Still keeping up appearances, he had to pretend to go home to look after the pocket-book, leaving the jubilant Mr. Hills to improve the shining hour with Miss Bradshaw.

Mr. Kemp, returning home at midnight—in a cab—found the young man waiting up for him, and, taking a seat on the edge of the table, listened unmoved to a word-picture of himself which seemed interminable. He was only moved to speech when Mr. Wright described him as a white-whiskered jezebel who was a disgrace to his sex, and then merely in the interests of natural science.

"Don't you worry," he said, as the other paused from exhaustion. "It won't be for long now."

"Long?" said Mr. Wright, panting. "First thing to-morrow morning you have a telegram calling you back—a telegram that must be minded. D'ye see?"

"No, I don't," said Mr. Kemp, plainly. "I'm not going back, never no more—never! I'm going to stop here and court Mrs. Bradshaw."

Mr. Wright fought for breath. "You—you can't!" he gasped.

"I'm going to have a try," said the old man. "I'm sick of going to sea, and it'll be a nice comfortable home for my old age. You marry Bella, and I'll marry her mother. Happy family!"

Mr. Wright, trembling with rage, sat down to recover, and, regaining his composure after a time, pointed out almost calmly the various difficulties in the way.

"I've thought it all out," said Mr. Kemp, nodding. "She mustn't know I'm not rich till after we're married; then I 'ave a letter from New Zealand saying I've lost all my money. It's just as easy to have that letter as the one you spoke of."

"And I'm to find you money to play the rich uncle with till you're married, I suppose," said Mr. Wright, in a grating voice, "and then lose Bella when Mrs. Bradshaw finds you've lost your money?"

Mr. Kemp scratched his ear. "That's your lookout," he said, at last.

"Now, look here," said Mr. Wright, with great determination. "Either you go and tell them that you've been telegraphed for—cabled is the proper word—or I tell them the truth."

"That'll settle you then," said Mr. Kemp.

"No more than the other would," retorted the young man, "and it'll come cheaper. One thing I'll take my oath of, and that is I won't give you another farthing; but if you do as I tell you I'll give you a quid for luck. Now, think it over."

Mr. Kemp thought it over, and after a vain attempt to raise the promised reward to five pounds, finally compounded for two, and went off to bed after a few stormy words on selfishness and ingratitude. He declined to speak to his host at breakfast next morning, and accompanied him in the evening with the air of a martyr going to the stake. He listened in stony silence to the young man's instructions, and only spoke when the latter refused to pay the two pounds in advance.

The news, communicated in halting accents by Mr. Kemp, was received with flattering dismay. Mrs. Bradshaw refused to believe her ears, and it was only after the information had been repeated and confirmed by Mr. Wright that she understood.

"I must go," said Mr. Kemp. "I've spent over eleven pounds cabling to-day; but it's all no good."

21

"But you're coming back?" said Mr. Hills.

"O' course I am," was the reply. "George is the only relation I've got, and I've got to look after him, I suppose. After all, blood is thicker than water."

"Hear, hear!" said Mrs. Bradshaw, piously.

"And there's you and Bella," continued Mr. Kemp; "two of the best that ever breathed."

The ladies looked down.

"And Charlie Hills; I don't know—I don't know *when* I've took such a fancy to anybody as I have to 'im. If I was a young gal—a single young gal—he's—the other half," he said, slowly, as he paused—"just the one I should fancy. He's a good-'arted, good-looking——"

"Draw it mild," interrupted the blushing Mr. Hills as Mr. Wright bestowed a ferocious glance upon the speaker.

"Clever, lively young fellow," concluded Mr. Kemp. "George!"

"Yes," said Mr. Wright.

"I'm going now. I've got to catch the train for Southampton, but I don't want you to come with me. I prefer to be alone. You stay here and cheer them up. Oh, and before I forget it, lend me a couple o' pounds out o' that fifty I gave you last night. I've given all my small change away."

22

He looked up and met Mr. Wright's eye; the latter, too affected to speak, took out the money and passed it over.

"We never know what may happen to us," said the old man, solemnly, as he rose and buttoned his coat. "I'm an old man and I like to have things ship-shape. I've spent nearly the whole day with my lawyer, and if anything 'appens to my old carcass it won't make any difference. I have left half my money to George; half of all I have is to be his."

In the midst of an awed silence he went round and shook hands.

"The other half," with his hand on the door—"the other half and my best gold watch and chain I have left to my dear young pal, Charlie Hills. Good-bye, Georgie!"